River
of
Hands

A Project of the
Canadian Cultural Society
of the Deaf

OTHER PUBLICATIONS OF THE LADDER AWARDS, CANADIAN DEAF HERITAGE PROJECT:

River of Hands: ASL Stories, (VHS/ CD Rom), Canadian Cultural Society of the Deaf, For the Record Productions
River of Hands: the Documentary, (VHS/CD Rom), Canadian Cultural Society of the Deaf, For the Record Productions

Copies can be purchased from:

The Canadian Cultural Society of the Deaf Bookstore, House 144, 11337-61 Avenue, Edmonton, Alberta, T6H 1M3

www.ccsdeaf.com, Email: ccsd@connect.ab.ca, TTY: (780) 430-9489, Fax: (780) 436-2599

$9.95 each plus applicable taxes, shipping & handling

Cover Illustration: COLLEEN TURNER

River of Hands

of

Hands

Deaf Heritage Stories

By
Symara Nichola Bonner
Jason Lee Brace
Kayla Marie Bradford
Sarah Rose Saumier-Barr

Illustrations by
Faim Poirier
Edward Tager
Cecilia Tung
Colleen Turner
Alan Yu

Second
Story
Press

Canadian Cataloguing in Publication Data

River of hands: deaf heritage stories

ISBN 1-896764-36-3

1. Deaf - Juvenile fiction. 2. Deaf, Writings of the (Canadian).*
3. Teenagers' Writings, Canadian (English).* 4. Children's stories, Canadian (English).* 5. Short stories, Canadian (English).*
I. Brace, Jason. II. Poirier, Faim.

PS8323.D35R58 2000   jC813'.010835208162   C00-932111-X
PZ5.R535 2000

*Second Story Press gratefully acknowledges the assistance of the Ontario Arts Council and the Canada Council for the Arts for our publishing program. We acknowledge the financial support of the Government of Canada through the Book Publishing Industry Development Program for our publishing activities.
We gratefully acknowledge the financial support of Human Resources Development Canada for this project.*

Book Design and Design Elements: Stephanie Martin

Printed and bound in Canada

Published by:
SECOND STORY PRESS
720 Bathurst Street, Suite 301
Toronto Canada M5S 2R4

Dedicated in memory of Christy Mackinnon
(1889-1981), author of Silent Observer.
She remains the sole Canadian Deaf author
of children's literature until the printing of this book.
We are grateful for her skill and honour the legacy
she left for us to continue!

Contents

A Fishy Story

Illustrator: EDWARD TAGER

By Jason Lee Brace

Once upon a time, Aaron and I wanted to go fishing. But we didn't know where to go. There didn't seem to be water anyplace close. There was no ocean, no lake, and no pond near where we lived.

After thinking and thinking and thinking some more, Aaron suggested, "Why don't we go to the pet store and try fishing in the tanks?"

While I knew there were lots of fish in the pet store, I was sure the owner wouldn't agree to Aaron's plan.

Finally, I got a brainstorm. Aaron and I would go fishing in the toilet. There was water in the bowl, And I figured it must lead to go to a place filled with fish.

We would need a very long line for the rod.

And worms.

Or a lure.

Now we were all ready.

Aaron and I both got chairs and carried them into the bathroom, so we could have a comfortable day of fishing. PERFECT!

I sat down facing Aaron and put the line into the toilet. Holding onto the rod, I nudged Aaron and nodded to the lever handle, "Please flush." He did.

Now the line goes all the way down, into the pipes and outside. We have no idea where it ends up. After a while, Aaron's head jerks back, and he nods, "Let's reel it in."

I reel and reel and reel. But when the line is finally out of the toilet, there are no fish at the end of it. We're disappointed, we pout, but we're not ready to give up. We try again.

No luck.

After thinking for a moment, Aaron signs, "Let's try my toilet. Maybe the pipes at our house go to a place where there are more fish."

We walk next door to Aaron's house, make sure his mom and dad are busy elsewhere, and again take a couple of chairs into the bathroom.

We put the line into the bowl and flush.

We wait as more and more of the line gets sucked into the pipes, to someplace where we hope there is a great big world of fish.

His hands flying impatiently, Aaron signs, "It's my turn to reel." He reels and reels and reels and something weird happens. The line begins to shake. Aaron can barely hold on. I grab him, and we pull together.

We pull.

The line tugs back.

We pull harder.

The line tugs back harder.

Finally, Aaron and I reel back as far as we can, holding tight to the rod. In an explosion of water, out flies the biggest fish we have ever seen. It's jumping and fighting us so hard that we don't know what to do.

The giant fish lands on the floor, sliding all over the place. We can't get a hold of it. Aaron tries to lie on top of it but I pull him off. I'm afraid he'll squish it too much.

I have a better idea. Let's put the fish in the bathtub. I motion to Aaron, and in one mighty grab, we lift the fish, place it into the tub, and turn on the taps.

Sitting back in the fishing chairs to get our breath, we have our first good look at our catch.

Aaron signs, "CHA CHA FISH," meaning it's so HUGE. "What do we do with it?"

"I don't know," I admit. "It's too big to cook, I think. Besides, I'll bet my mom won't let me eat anything that comes out of a toilet bowl."

"My mom either," Aaron agrees. "Let's take a picture to show our monster-sized fish to everybody, and then put the fish back in the toilet."

"Great idea! Let's do it right now."

After taking an instant photograph, Aaron and I breathe deeply and lift the squirming fish out of the tub and into the toilet bowl. We both say goodbye to the fish, and then I flush. Most of the fish disappears down the toilet, but not the tail. Oops!

"It's stuck," signs Aaron, his eyes wide. "Let's flush again."

We flush. Nothing. I sure hope his parents don't come along right now, imagine their stamping footsteps coming.

We flush again. No good.

We flush once more, but it's still stuck. What are we going to do?

Finally, I have another brainstorm. "Let's get the plunger."

Careful not to hurt the fish, we plunge as hard as we can. Finally the fish disappears down through the pipes and back to its fish home in the water far away.

Exhausted but happy, Aaron and I can hardly believe what just happened. We look at the picture of our giant toilet catch. Sitting back in our bathroom fishing chairs, we smile at each other.

Aaron and I just love to go fishing.

What does "signing" mean?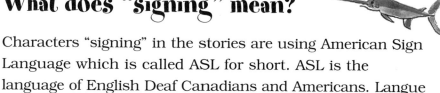

Characters "signing" in the stories are using American Sign Language which is called ASL for short. ASL is the language of English Deaf Canadians and Americans. Langue des Signes Québecoise, called LSQ for short, is the language of French Deaf Canadians. Both have their own vocabulary, grammar, and social rules for how they are used.

Love Fishing

Fish

Bathroom

Toilet

Worm

by Sarah Rose Saumier-Barr

Calamine

Calamine and Ralph Frider had never gone on a vacation, not once in their twenty-five years of marriage.

They were always so busy taking their three kids to school, bringing them home, helping them with their homework, and making sure they had lots of fun in their spare time. Calamine and Ralph loved their busy life. But then something happened.

One day, they found themselves alone in their home. All their children had grown up and moved away. For the first time in many, many years, Calamine and Ralph didn't know what to do with themselves. No one was asking them to pick up this or that, or to take them here or there. Calamine and Ralph were bored.

After sitting around for days and days and then weeks and weeks, Calamine jumped out of her chair and began to shake Ralph, who was snoozing in front of the television.

"Ralph, I have a great idea. Why not take a vacation?"

"Oh, goody!" signed Ralph. "You make the plans." And he went back to sleep with a big smile.

Calamine sent an e-mail to the travel agent, read a huge stack of books about places to visit, and finally made a decision. She found Ralph in the hammock in the back yard.

"We're going to the Beached Inn on Balmy Bay!"

"Oh, goody!" agreed Ralph. "You pack." He pulled his sunhat down over his eyes.

While Calamine found the suitcases, and filled them with bathing suits, shorts, sunscreen, and sandals, Ralph took a little nap.

"I'm ready," signed Calamine as she shook him awake.

"Oh, goody!" he answered. "You drive." He tucked himself into the passenger seat, with a comfy pillow.

So Calamine drove and drove and drove some more, going up mountains and down valleys, until they arrived at the Beached Inn on Balmy Bay.

She parked the car and poked Ralph in the ribs. "We're here," Calamine woke the snoring Ralph.

"Oh, goody!" Ralph responded. "You carry the bags."

"No, you carry them," retorted Calamine, jabbing a finger under his nose and jumping out of the car. "I'm on vacation!"

Surprised, but happy to be doing something instead of snoozing all the time, Ralph put a suitcase under each arm, and followed Calamine up to their room. It was huge, with a big bed, a big dresser, and a big window looking over Balmy Bay.

"Let's go swimming," signed Calamine, looking at the beautiful beach outside.

"Oh, goody!" answered Ralph, but instead of saying "you unpack," he began going through the suitcases himself, digging out their bathing suits, shorts, sunscreen, and sandals.

Calamine and Ralph had a wonderful time swimming, tanning, going to a restaurant, watching a video, eating snacks, and taking a long, long walk. By bedtime they were pooped. Not since their children had left home had they done so much in one day.

So Calamine signed to Ralph, "Dear, you and I can sleep as late as we want, because no one is here to bother us."

"Oh, goody!" thought Ralph and instead of telling Calamine to hang the *Do Not Disturb* sign on the door-knob, he did it himself. Calamine and Ralph barely got into bed before they fell into a deep, deep sleep. They were so tired that they didn't wake up for breakfast. When Missy, the very considerate maid, came by to clean their room, she saw the *Do Not Disturb* sign and decided to come back later.

But Calamine and Ralph were so tired that they slept through lunch as well. Missy kept coming back, but the sign was still up. She returned at one o'clock, two o'clock, three o'clock and even four o'clock and five o'clock but the *Do Not Disturb* sign was still hanging from the doorknob.

What should she do?

Missy began to worry. What if the people in the room were sick? She knocked gently on the door. No answer. She knocked harder. Still nothing.

No one at the hotel had any idea that Calamine and Ralph were both Deaf.

After knocking as hard as she could and getting no response, Missy ran down the stairs to get Big Bob, the manager of the Beached Inn on Balmy Bay. Big Bob pounded on the door until all the people up and down the hallway looked out to see what was wrong. All except Calamine and Ralph — they were still sound asleep.

After shouting and banging as loud as he could, Big Bob decided that something must be wrong. He called the fire station. He called the police. He called an ambulance. And what happened then? Chaos.

Wheeil, Wheeil, went the sirens. *Flash* went the red lights on the ambulance, fire engine, and police cars. *Clang* went the bells and *blap* went the bass vibrations of the air horns. The racket scared everyone in Balmy Bay — except Calamine and Ralph, who just kept sleeping.

WHEEEIL

WHEEL

One of the firefighters pulled out a ladder, and climbed up to their window and banged and banged but the two tired sleepers slept on. Then the firefighter used an axe to break the window, and climbed inside.

Soon a whole roomful of people from the fire department, police department, and ambulance service were crowded around Calamine and Ralph, talking and shouting. The two went on sleeping quietly.

Finally, a paramedic touched Ralph on his neck, to check for a pulse, and he sat bolt upright. This woke Calamine, and she sat up too, shocked at all the people surrounding their bed.

She waved her hands in the air, "What's wrong?"

One by one, the people who had come to rescue Ralph and Calamine came to understand that they were simply Deaf.

Soon, everyone was laughing at the misunderstanding. The police wrote in their little black notebooks and drove away. The firefighters picked up their axes and apologized for breaking the window. The paramedics packed their medical kits and left. And Calamine and Ralph wrote Big Bob a list of things he could do so that, next time, he wouldn't need the fire department, police department, and the ambulance to help him serve his Deaf guests.

Big Bob thanked Calamine and Bob for their suggestions, and said they could stay at the Beached Inn at Balmy Bay for free whenever they wanted.

How do you think Ralph replied? Yes, you're right. "Oh, goody!" he signed, and went back to sleep.

Did You Ever WONDER?

What was it like before flashing lights for doorbells were invented?

◆ People would use the back door. It was never locked. They were allowed to open the door and then stamp or bang on the floor. We would feel the vibration of the banging and stamping and come to see who was at the door.

◆ We created our own homemade technology by using a 12-volt transmitter on the front door, adding a wire to a lamp and when someone rang the doorbell, the lamp would flash.

◆ People would use a flashlight to shine on the windows hoping to attract attention. Sometimes they would use their car high beams to flash on and off towards the windows.

BUT...

by Kayla Marie
Bradford

Bobby

and his wife, Janice, live in a small house in an even smaller town. They have a son named Matt who is eleven years old. Like his parents Matt has been Deaf all his life.

Bobby has a great job. He fixes weird wired things for the electric company. Janice works in a bakery, which gives her a chance to eat more desserts than are really good for her. She always complains about her weight, but no one pays attention to her any more, since she enjoys those sweets more than she minds not being skinny. And Matt loves going to a very good school for Deaf kids (where he sometimes gets into trouble for his joke-making).

Eveyone finds it surprising that Bobby has never been late for work in twenty-five years. He gets up early for a good reason. In order to get to the office, he must pass a railway crossing. If he's even a little bit late, the crossing gates come down and he has to wait until a super-duper, extra-long train goes by.

Luckily, Bobby has never had a problem getting up in time. One day his boss, Mike, even gave him an award for his promptness. Curious about Bobby's punctuality, Mike signed, "How do you get to work so early?"

Bobby smiled and answered, his hands flying through the air, "Well, after all these years, I've trained myself to wake up at a certain time. Also, I have an extra-bright clock light. Besides, Janice moves around so much when she sleeps that she kicks me every few minutes."

But the very next day, disaster struck. Bobby was up late the night before, reading, so he slept in. Can you believe that the clock light also broke that same night? And Janice was visiting her sister, so there was no one to kick him awake.

Finally, Matt realized that his father had overslept. He shook Bobby awake. "HURRY UP! You will be late for work!" Bobby was frantic. He did his best, jumping straight into his pants and out the door. No 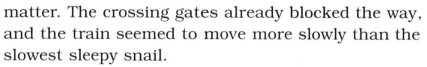 matter. The crossing gates already blocked the way, and the train seemed to move more slowly than the slowest sleepy snail.

Bobby could do nothing but wait and wait and wait some more. Finally, when the train had passed, he looked to see if the gates were going up. They weren't. Bobby, pulling his hair out by now, blasted the car horn so that the crossing gate attendant would hurry and raise the gates.

Nothing happened.

Looking around, Bobby saw that the man was asleep in a nearby shed. Jumping out of the car, he banged and banged and banged on the window until the man, whose name was George, awoke. Confused and still groggy, George said, "What? *What?*" Bobby signed back hastily, explaining the problem. But George didn't understand American Sign Language and it looked to him as though Bobby was trying to tell him something, gesturing and mouthing the word "BUT."

George raised his hand and asked, "What?"

Bobby signed back, but again all George could see was this.

He looked Bobby in the eye and said, "What do you want?"

Sure that he had discovered the solution to their miscommunication, Bobby took out a pen and paper and wrote in big, big letters "BUT." He thought this would clear up everything. But again George didn't understand.

What a shock!

No matter how many times Bobby mouthed the word "But," or wrote it down, George still couldn't figure out what he was trying to say. Bobby realized he was going to be late for work for the first time ever. He was sad for a moment and then tried to look for the funny side.

With this guy, he might get a day off and a great story to tell his friends.

But would the gate ever "BUT"?

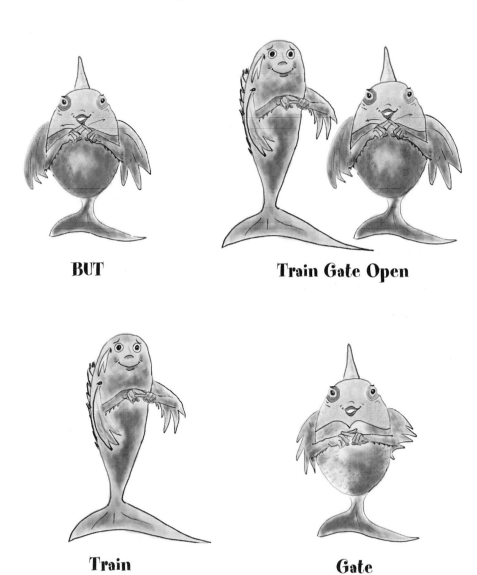

BUT

Train Gate Open

Train

Gate

Did You Ever WONDER?

How did we wake up before flashing alarms or vibrating alarms were invented?

♦ Drink a glass of water before bedtime and you will wake up naturally due to "nature's call" (This is still in use even today)!

♦ A clock was attached to a battery with the lamp attached to the same battery. This was our home invention.

♦ Rapping on the bed by the supervisor at the residential school.

♦ At home we were awakened by our relatives.

♦ An alarm clock would be placed under the pillow.

♦ A visit to the Gallaudet University Archives unlocked nuggets into our lifestyle at the turn of the 19th century. It revealed an idea for a "tactile" alarm clock (circa 1898) — at the pre-set time, an alarm clock outfitted with an outstretched rod would drop a sandbag on the sleeping Deaf person (The Silent Echo / Gallaudet University Archives cited in Carbin, 1996).* That may be the reason why Deaf people were very punctual at their places of employment in those days!

* Carbin, C.F. (1996). *Deaf Heritage in Canada.* Whitby, Ontario: McGraw-Hill Ryerson Limited, p.444.

Unlucky
Charm

Illustrator: CECILIA TUNG

by Symara Nichola Bonner

Leoain

Leoain pressed her finger down on the television remote control button and watched the channels flicker by. So many channels and not a thing to watch. She was really supposed to be studying for a test. Yuck!

She stretched her arms high above her head. She couldn't believe how incredibly bored she was. She yawned and thought she would close her eyes for just a moment, and then start doing some real studying.

When she opened her eyes again, Leoain was no longer alone in her room. Somehow she was with her best friend, Samara, walking through a creaky wooden door into a shop on the village road. The store was tiny. They'd almost walked past it until Leoain noted a sign hanging above the door: BEAD ALL THAT YOU CAN BEAD.

"Strange," Samara signed to her friend. "I've been on this street a million times, and I've never seen this place before."

The girls walked into the dimly lit store. There was no one in sight. Then Samara signed, "I feel someone coming." A woman appeared from behind two curtains along the back wall. She was small and elderly, peering over half glasses, with an unpleasant scowl on her face. She wore a long robe, and lots of beaded necklaces around her neck.

"Yes?" the woman mumbled, so that the girls could hardly read her lips. "What do you want?

Leoain swallowed hard. She was ready to answer, but this woman did not understand sign language. So she used gestures indicating, "Oh, um, we're just here to look."

The woman didn't reply. She pursed her lips and disappeared back through the curtains.

"What's with her?" Samara asked in a whispery way by signing low, small and close to the body so that only Leoain could see.

Leoain shrugged. Her face screwed up. "Dunno. She gives me the creeps. Big time!"

"Yeah, but check out all these cool beads!" Samara signed excitedly, gazing around the store. There were more beads here than she had seen in her whole life.

"I know! Let's make matching friendship bracelets!"

"Good idea!" Leoain agreed.

The problem was that there were so many beads, the girls couldn't choose. Finally, Leoain suggested that they ask the store owner for help.

"Hello?" Leoain waved her hand toward the back room to get her attention.

"I'm right here, young lady," the woman yelled as she touched Leoain on the shoulder.

"Oh! You startled me!" Leoain indicated, putting her hands to her chest.

The woman barely blinked. "What do you want?" her face wrinkled as she muttered.

Leoain took a breath, shoved her hands into her pockets, brought out a notepad and pen and somehow found the courage to write. "We were wondering if you had any more beads, maybe ones that are really special."

"What's the matter?" the woman demanded. "You don't see anything you like? Never mind. I think I know what you're looking for."

She parted the curtains and disappeared once again. Leoain and Samara barely had time to exchange looks before she came back. In her hands she held an old wooden box.

"Here," she grumbled. "Look through these."

The girls lifted the lid and gasped. They had never seen such beautifully cool beads before. The brilliant colours and the intricate designs were unbelievable.

"They're all so amazing! How much are they?" wrote Leoain.

"They're free," said the woman, snapping her fingers and shaking her head to indicate that there was no charge.

"FREE, COOL!" The girls couldn't understand. "But why?" questioned Leoain.

The store owner sighed. "There's something I guess you should know about those beads. I got them from a man many years ago. He said that they were cursed and he didn't want them anywhere near him."

Samara and Leoain were astonished. Cursed!

"Cursed," the woman repeated and wrote, "Jinxed. Hexed. Bad luck. That's what he said. He told me his wife got them at a yard sale. The owner was giving the beads away, anxious to get rid of them. The wife made a necklace out of them and wore it all the time, but then terrible things kept happening to her. She was convinced it was the beads. Anyway, he told me that he'd tried to destroy them but they kept reappearing."

"What happened to his wife?" Leoain scribbled.

"She got very sick with some mysterious illness. I never heard if she recovered."

"That's awful!" signed Samara. The two girls stared at the pretty beads on the counter.

"Look, kids, I'm really busy today," the store owner said suddenly. "Do you want the beads or not?"

Leoain looked at the beads and then at Samara. How could beads be cursed? The story was totally ridiculous. Maybe the old woman liked to scare kids with her weird stories. "We'll take them," she motioned finally. "We're not afraid of any dumb curse."

"Are you sure, Leoain?" Samara signed nervously.

"DEFINITELY. We'll take them," she indicated to the

owner by pointing to the beads and looking up at the woman and nodding. "And we'll take our chances," Leoain wrote on a note she handed to the shop keeper with a laugh.

No one laughed with her.

As she sat in class the next day, Leoain thought that this was turning out to be the worst day of her life.

It had started out okay. Both she and Samara loved their new friendship bracelets, and many girls in her class had said they couldn't wait to make their own bead bracelets.

But now everything was going wrong. First, she'd misplaced her knapsack with her wallet and schoolbooks. Then, something bizarre had happened; Samara had been taken to the hospital with a horrible rash. In the middle of class Samara had started itching. When Samara turned around to tell Leoain, Leoain had seen that her friend's face and neck were full of gross, ugly bumps. And poor Samara couldn't stop scratching. The teacher had rushed Samara down to the nurse, who had sent her to the hospital.

Now, something even stranger had happened. Leoain had just learned that she was getting an F on a very important test. Returning her paper her teacher had commented, "I'm surprised at you."

"But, Ms. Barton, I studied hard for this!" Leoain had replied, but Ms. Barton had just looked at her severely.

Leoain looked over the exam. The answers were all wrong — she could see that now. How could this have happened? She had known the right answers, but there was no way to prove it now. This F was going to hurt her final grade in the class.

Walking home, Leoain wondered what was happening. She wanted to cry. This day was turning out to be a nightmare. The only good thing about it was her beautiful bracelet. She looked at it fondly, running her fingers over the beads ...

Suddenly, she felt a shock through her body. How could she have forgotten? The old woman had warned them. She'd said the beads were cursed. Leoain's heart pounded.

What if it was true? she wondered. What if everything that happened today had been because of the cursed beads? Leoain could barely breathe. That has to be it! she thought to herself. Samara was right! I should have believed the old woman! We have to get rid of these beads!

Frantically, she ripped the bracelet from her wrist. The cord broke, sending the beads sailing through the air. Without a moment to waste, she ran home, grabbed the TTY, and dialed the hospital.

"Samara!" she typed into the TTY when her friend answered. "It's the bracelet! It's cursed! Take off the bracelet!"

Samara was so swollen and itchy that she could barely move but she took off the bracelet. Weakly she promised that she would call Leoain later.

Leoain sat at home hoping desperately that her friend would get better now. She waited for ages, and then finally her TTY light flashed in her room.

"Leoain, it worked!" Samara typed into the TTY. "I think the curse is broken. The rash — it's going away! **GA**."

Leoain's heart pumped wildly. "Samara! That's great! Now throw the bracelet away for good! Bye! **GA** to **SK**."

Leoain hung up the phone and collapsed onto her bed. Her heart slowly stopped pounding and her breathing returned to normal. Everything was going to be okay! But now she was just so tired ...

When Leoain woke up, she was in her room with her schoolbooks all around. Had her big test happened? Had she been dreaming? Were Samara's rash and the bead bracelet and the curse all for real? Ready to call Samara, Leoain stopped and thought for a moment.

Maybe it was better not to know.

Did You Ever WONDER?

What is a TTY?

A TTY is a teletypewriter. It is a small, portable piece of equipment similar to a typewriter with a keyboard, message display, and a place to put the telephone handset on. Some also have a paper print-out. Two Deaf people with a TTY can reach each other, or a TTY can be used to call a hearing person who doesn't have a TTY by using the Bell Relay Service. The message is typed to the Bell Relay operator, who passes the message verbally to the person without the TTY; then the response is passed back through the relay service — or vice versa. Bell Relay can be reached by dialing 1-800-855-0511 (voice) or 711 (TTY). Of course, when both people have TTY the conversation flows much more smoothly and children and adults can enjoy their direct conversation.

When did the TTY network begin in Canada?

◆ In the early 1970's.

How did we communicate without the phone before the invention of the TTY?

◆ We would write letters on Monday and mail them immediately. In those days, the mail system was far better! The person would get their letter on Tuesday or Wednesday and mail back a response right away. If a visit was to occur that weekend, our plans would be all set!

◆ We asked a neighbour to make a phone call. Often we would have the number of our Deaf friend's next door neighbour, so our neighbour could call their neighbour!

◆ We had a gathering time and place, usually at a friend's place and Deaf friends would know when it would be held, such as every Wednesday at 7:00 p.m. Deaf people would meet there and discuss plans for the weekend or activities for the organization.

◆ We'd drive over and hope the person was home. If they were not home, oh well ...

◆ **GA** – Go ahead meaning it's your turn to type.

◆ **SK** – Stop keying, meaning it's time to hang up.

Authors

SYMARA NICHOLA BONNER, age 17, lives in Mississauga,

Ontario. She has won several student awards and the Optimist International Communications Contest in 1997. She loves writing letters and going out with friends. Her dream is to continue her education to become an actress as well as a writer.

JASON LEE BRACE, age 14, lives in Chance Cove,

Newfoundland. He has received several student awards for reading, language, and science, as well as the Ladder Award. Jason enjoys riding his bike and writing funny stories. He hopes to become a wealthy man in the future!

KAYLA MARIE BRADFORD, age 12, lives in Edmonton,

Alberta. She enjoys using the computer, drawing, writing short stories, playing basketball and soccer. At school she has won best sports person and a communication award. She hopes to become an elementary school teacher for Deaf students.

SARAH ROSE SAUMIER-BARR, age 12, lives in

Edmonton, Alberta. A former winner of the Alberta School for the Deaf Best Story Award, Sarah loves reading poetry, suspence fiction, and humour. She also loves basketball, soccer and running. Her dream is to become a teacher for Deaf students.

ILLUSTRATORS

FAIM POIRIER, age 25, lives in Milton, Ontario, and  aspires to go to art college. She has designed logos for T-shirts, newspaper and flyers for the Ontario Camp for the Deaf. She loves animals and enjoys volunteering with the Humane Society. She likes her drawings to make others laugh!

EDWARD TAGER, age 71, lives in Dollard Des Omeraux,  Quebec, and has worked as a technical illustrator for many years. He has recieved recognition for his fine technical abilities. He enjoys researching to make his illustrations as technically accurate as possible. He hopes to do freelance illustration.

CECILIA TUNG, age 18, lives in Vancouver, British  Columbia. She has been involved in school council as well as writing newspaper articles. She aspires to become a teacher in the arts and wishes to develop her own art abilities to provide a "voice" for Deaf people through visual media.

 COLLEEN TURNER, age 29, lives in Eastport Booth Bay, Newfoundland, with her husband and daughter. She loves art, drama, and trail riding her horse. She thinks it is important to be proud of your talents as a Deaf person. Recently, she was asked to paint a mural for the Town of Eastport homecoming 2000 celebrations. She aspires to work full time as an artist.

 ALAN YU, age 21, lives in Laval, Quebec. A former student of the Mackay Centre, Alan won the Ladder Award for illustration in 1999 as well as several other school awards. He is now focusing his efforts on comic drawing and illustration. He aspires to be an artist by looking for the challenge in each project.

AFTERWORD

Every good story has a story behind it. The story behind this book began in 1998. We were working for The Canadian Cultural Society of Deaf with TVOntario developing an American Sign Language (ASL) and English Literature videotape series called, Freckles and Popper for children ages 4–7. In one segment of those tapes we wanted to share English stories with Deaf characters and Deaf cultural experience written by Deaf people. Our intent was to share those books in ASL. We soon discovered that there were none published in this country! Deaf experience is absent from our children's literature! If you look on the shelves of any bookstore or library you will find virtually no Canadian-produced children's literature by a Deaf Canadian either in book form or signed in American Sign Language on videotape. We found one children's book, *Silent Observer*, written and illustrated by a Deaf woman, Christy MacKinnon. In it, she shares the charming story of her life growing up as a little girl on the family farm and at her residential school in 19th century Nova Scotia. Christy's manuscript was discovered after her death by her niece and published in the United States.

With virtually no Canadian-published children's Deaf literature, we decided to establish the Ladder Awards ™ Program (initially known as the Deaf Heritage Literature Awards). It was our good fortune to receive financial support from Human Resources Development Canada, and consultation from Kids Netword. By 1999 The Ladder Awards™ Program was born as a project of the Canadian Cultural Society of the Deaf. Its purpose was to increase the small amount of published Canadian children's ASL and Deaf literature that exists today. It simultaneously provided an opportunity for new Deaf authors, storytellers and illustrators to emerge from across the country. *River of Hands: Deaf Heritage Stories* is an anthology of stories created by Deaf authors and Deaf illustrators as a result of The Ladder Awards™ Program.

The Ladder Awards ™ process is described in the videotape, "River of Hands: A Documentary." Deaf Canadians of all ages were invited to submit their written stories, ASL videotapes and illustrations to The Ladder Awards ™ competition in the spring of 1999. The winners of the Ladder Awards ™ range in age from seven to seventy five and come from all across Canada ... from Vancouver to Newfoundland! This book is the result of the written and illustration selections of that competition. The videotape, River of Hands: ASL Stories is the result of the ASL section of the Ladder Awards ™ Program. Four authors and five illustrators were selected from the competition. Their work is the basis of this book. Judges for the written stories were: Sue Chekeris, teacher/librarian and chair of the elementary picture book committee, Peel Board of education; Heather Gibson, vice principal, E.C. Drury School for the Deaf; Phoebe Gilman, award-winning children's picturebook author and illustrator; Dr. David Mason, professor, Deaf Education Teacher Preparation Program, York University; and Margie Wolfe, Publisher, Second Story

Press. Judges for the illustrations included: Regent Gendron, graduate in Studio Art from Gallaudet University, who serves on the GOLD Board supporting adult literacy in the Deaf community; Laura D. Walker, award-winning fashion illustrator; and Steve Quinlan, Assistant Dean, Faculty of Design, Ontario College of Art and Design.

The author and illustrator winners of the Ladder Awards™ received an intensive weekend of workshops along with their ASL winner counterparts. Heather Gibson and Laura Walker served as consultants for Deaf heritage content during the workshops for written stories and illustrations respectively. Following the workshops, the authors were mentored by Margie Wolfe and Peter Carver via e-mail. Stories went through an editorial process until they evolved to what you read today. The essential story elements remain as they were initially expressed, preserving the story line, intent, and cultural influence of the authors.

We were also fortunate to have the Ontario College of Art and Design in Toronto, Ontario provide an intensive week of illustration training in January 2000. The illustrators were mentored by renowned illustrators such as Phoebe Gilman, Ian Wallace, Ruth Ohi, Maryann Kovalski and Brenda Clark. Each winner was assigned one of these mentors and they worked on, obtained feedback, and revised their colour illustrations via express mail across the country.

This book is the first of its kind for Canadian children's literature! The stories, *But* and *Zzzzzz* are traditional Deaf folktales passed down from generation to generation of Deaf people through American Sign Language. To our knowledge, they have never been recorded on videotape or in print. *A Fishy Story* and *Unlucky Charm* are original stories created by the authors. These stories are just the beginning. The community's sharing of culturally rich stories will grow in books over time.

Much thanks go to Margie Wolfe, Phoebe Gilman, and Steve Quinlan who helped us tremendously to see this dream become a reality. Our thanks also go to Heather Hawthorn who was a wonderful interpreter for the many people we worked with.

Our thanks are especially extended to the many Deaf Canadians who participated in this program and to the contributors of this book who worked hard to expand Deaf experience in Canadian children's literature. The real story behind the book is that Deaf people have been sharing stories with each other for generations. We are thrilled to have some of those stories shared here with you now through this book!

Hope you enjoyed them! Hands waving – *Pah*!*

Joanne Cripps   Anita Small, Ed.D.
Project Director   Head of Research & Development
The Ladder Awards ™   The Ladder Awards ™

Canadian Deaf Heritage Project
Canadian Cultural Society of the Deaf

* *"Pah"* is how we express "success at last" in the Deaf community.